MingLing

Written by: Stephen Cosgrove
Illustrated by: Robin James

A Serendipity™ Book

PRICE STERN SLOAN
Los Angeles

ISBN: 0-8431-0592-5

20 19 18 17 16 15 14 13 12 11 10

Dedicated to William Russe and all the Pandas of the world. May they all live forever in the magical Panda Pines.

Stephen

West of west and east of east lay the forever forest called the Panda Pines. Because of the gentle rains, plants grew there in great profusion. Rice nut trees and bamboo thickets shimmered in the magical mists that surrounded the Panda Pines.

As you can well imagine, this forest of bamboo provided a marvelous shelter for feathered birds of every kind, including cockatiels and cockatoos—and even a pair of parrots. All of them would flutter and flitter above and about the thicket, chittering and chattering their melodic songs.

Other than the birds, the only creature that lived there was a rumbly, grumbly Panda bear called Ming Ling. Ming Ling had two passions in life, to eat and to sleep. She wasn't grouchy by nature, but the birds of the thicket were eating up her food, and robbing her of her rest, to boot.

It seemed the birds were eating all of Ming Ling's pine nuts, her favorite thing to eat. Then they would sit in the trees after they ate, singing at the top of their feathery lungs. That would wake and frustrate the poor, hungry Panda even more.

One special morning, when it would have felt so good just to sleep another hour or two, the birds started singing and flapping their wings against the bamboo leaves, making the loudest racket you have ever heard. With a "Ruuff!" and a "Whuuff!" Ming Ling woke up abruptly.

"Why can't they wake up when I wake up?" she grumbled as she rubbed the sleep from her eyes. "What I need is a bird who will talk when I talk, walk when I walk, and, most of all, sleep when I sleep!" With that she sat on her haunches and roared to the trees, scaring a bird or two. Ming Ling knew she was going to have just another really bad day.

Because she couldn't sleep as long as she wanted, or eat all that she wished, Ming Ling became more and more cranky. She stomped around looking for pine nuts, getting grumblier and grumblier. Whenever she was just as cranky as she could be, the birds always started to sing a happy song. In a furious rage she would grab some branches in her mighty paws and shake them like a whip in the wind. I don't know if you have ever tried to sing and hold on to a branch at the same time, but the birds were finding it extremely difficult.

Ming Ling was so bearish that she began chasing and snapping at them with her teeth. She never caught one (and probably wouldn't know what to do if she did), but once or twice a bird's happy fluttering turned into frightened flittering and a feather or two graced the corners of Ming Ling's mouth as the bird escaped.

One day all of the birds, including the cockatiels and cockatoos, decided that they could stand no more. They packed up their nests, and together they all flew away. The silence that followed was like a golden blanket to Ming Ling, who wrapped herself in the delicious hush. Peacefully she ate and ate tender bamboo shoots and leaves. It was so absolutely still that she almost started to giggle once or twice. But that would have broken the warm, gentle stillness of the day.

It was so perfectly quiet that when she finished eating her fill she curled into a soft furry ball and, with no one or no bird to distract her, fell fast asleep.

Minutes turned to hours, hours turned to days, days turned to weeks. Suddenly the peace and quiet of the thicket began to press on Ming Ling's ears. Just as the birds had made too much noise, the silence hung heavy on her shoulders.

She wandered throughout Panda Pines, searching high and low for even one bird, but none could be found. Finally, as Ming Ling gave up, resigned to her fate, she spied a rather plump, red parrot sitting on a bamboo branch. She looked at the parrot. The parrot looked at her. Neither spoke a word.

Finally, Ming Ling could take the silence no more and eagerly said, "Do you speak?"

The parrot cocked its head to one side and, staring at Ming Ling with one silly eye, said, "Do you speak?"

Ming Ling slowly scratched her head and said, "Well, of course . . . but do you speak?"

The parrot paced from one end of the branch to the other and said, "Well, of course . . . but do you speak?"

Ming Ling growled, "You're being silly!"

Then the parrot growled, "You're being silly!"

Ming Ling's eyes opened wide with amazement. She had found the perfect bird. A bird who would sleep when she slept and talk when she talked, and say the words she loved to hear—her own.

"This is just great!" Ming Ling thought to herself. "This is my kind of bird." She began to walk slowly around the tree as the parrot mimicked her every move. "Panda bears are great!" she snickered out loud.

The parrot, true to his name, snickered right back, "Panda bears are great!"

"And Ming Ling is the greatest!" she laughed into her furry paw.

"And Ming Ling is the greatest!" the parrot laughed into its feathered wing.

With a smile as wide as the Panda Pines, Ming Ling, with the parrot waddling right behind, giggled her way into the forest.

The next day, after the sun had been up for an hour or more, Ming Ling stretched in the warm leaves that were her nest. "What a gorgeous morning," she yawned.

Above her head she heard feathers rustle, and a squawking voice yawned right back, "What a gorgeous morning."

So it went from day to day with Ming Ling talking on and on and the parrot repeating her every word.

As the days wore on, Ming Ling got just a little bit upset about their conversations. Though they talked on and on throughout the day, it didn't seem that the parrot was adding anything. Finally, one afternoon as Ming Ling was getting a drink down at the stream (as usual the parrot was doing the same), the Panda shouted loudly, "You dumb creature! Why don't you climb a tree and sing or something?"

The parrot, its feathers ruffled, shouted just as loudly, "You dumb creature! Why don't you climb a tree and sing or something?"

Ming Ling's eyes widened in anger and she screamed, "If you repeat what I say one more time, I'll eat you for dessert, you ball of feathered fluff!"

For the first time in a long time the parrot didn't repeat her statement. The air was thick with silence.

The parrot fluttered up into a tree and looked down at the angry, confused Panda bear. "What do you want, bear? First you want silence, then you don't, but now you do."

Sheepishly, Ming Ling sat and gazed at the ground. "I don't know. I thought I wanted it quiet, but that was boring. Then, I thought I just wanted to hear someone talk when I talked, and now I don't know what I want." She paused, deep in thought. "Maybe if the birds all came back . . ."

"Well," said the parrot, "they'll never come back if all you're going to do is roar at them!"

"Yeah, but they make so much noise, and I need a lot of sleep!"

"Hmmm." The parrot paced on a branch, thinking out loud. "With a bit of cooperation and a pinch of compromise I think you both can survive."

From that day forward, whenever Ming Ling wished for silence she did nothing more than stuff bamboo leaves in her ears. The birds were so happy singing without interruption that they carried great piles of pine nuts and the most tender leaves for her to eat when she woke from her afternoon naps.

And sometimes, when Ming Ling wasn't looking and couldn't hear, the plump, red parrot mimicked her every word.

IF YOU LIVE IN A FOREST
AND DON'T KNOW
HOW TO SHARE IT,
REMEMBER A PANDA
NAMED MING LING
AND A VERY SILLY PARROT.

Serendipity™ Books

Written by Stephen Cosgrove
Illustrated by Robin James

Enjoy all the delightful books in the Serendipity Series:

BANGALEE	LITTLE MOUSE ON THE PRAIRIE
BUTTERMILK	MAUI-MAUI
BUTTERMILK BEAR	MEMILY
CAP'N SMUDGE	MING LING
CATUNDRA	MINIKIN
CRABBY GABBY	MISTY MORGAN
CREOLE	MORGAN AND ME
CRICKLE-CRACK	MORGAN AND YEW
DRAGOLIN	MORGAN MINE
THE DREAM TREE	MORGAN MORNING
FANNY	THE MUFFIN MUNCHER
FEATHER FIN	MUMKIN
FLUTTERBY	NITTER PITTER
FLUTTERBY FLY	PERSNICKITY
GABBY	PISH POSH
GLITTERBY BABY	RAZ-MA-TAZ
THE GNOME FROM NOME	RHUBARB
GRAMPA-LOP	SASSAFRAS
HUCKLEBUG	SERENDIPITY
IN SEARCH OF THE SAVEOPOTOMAS	SHIMMEREE
JAKE O'SHAWNASEY	SNAFFLES
JINGLE BEAR	SNIFFLES
KARTUSCH	SQUEAKERS
KIYOMI	TEE-TEE
LEO THE LOP	TRAFALGAR TRUE
LEO THE LOP TAIL TWO	TRAPPER
LEO THE LOP TAIL THREE	WHEEDLE ON THE NEEDLE

The above books, and many others, can be bought wherever books are sold, or may be ordered directly from the publisher.

PRICE STERN SLOAN
360 North La Cienega Boulevard, Los Angeles, California 90048